Nancy

The Sacrifice of Aeros
Willow Asteria

Willow Asteria

Copyright © 2025 by Willow Asteria

All rights reserved.

No portion of this book may be reproduced in any form without written permission from the publisher or author, except as permitted by U.S. copyright law.

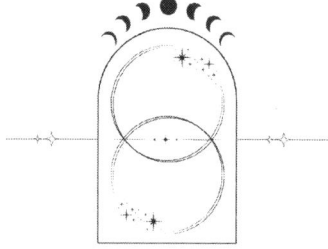

Content Warning

Please be advised that this book may not be suitable for all audiences.

This book contains sexual content, strict religious upbringing, death, blood, graphic violence, and other topics some readers may not find suitable.

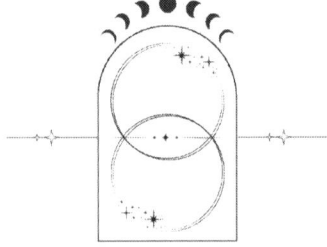

Realms of Elswyth

In the land of Elswyth, six portals exist that lead to the fae realms.

Orilon. Irolyth. Alari. Aeros. Khaldon. Tarak.

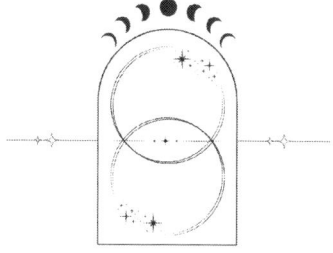

Prologue

Sage and rosemary filled my nose as I entered the sanctum. My knees buckled under me as I walked down the aisle. Looking down, I stared at my white shoes and the red runner through my thin veil. I focused on my breathing as I took one step after another. All eyes were on me, judging my every movement. Today was the most important day of my entire life.

My eighteenth birthday, and the day I would make my vows to The Mother.

She was the queen of our gods, and everyone who lived in the sanctuary on the small island of Varia pledged themselves to Her. Unlike my other sisters, I was raised within the sanctuary, and I worshiped her since I was little.

I should be happy to make these vows to Her. Instead, I felt ashamed of the apprehension I had. My entire life had been spent within the walls of the sanctuary. There had only been a few occasions I traveled into the town that was also on this small island.

What if there was a whole world waiting for me beyond the sea? What if I was meant for more than being shut away from the rest of the world?

Reaching up, I gripped my white pendant necklace as I approached the altar. It always brought me peace, and I hoped it wouldn't fail me now. I raised my gaze and looked at the Elder through my veil. She stood behind the altar, looking somehow more perfect than usual. The Elder strived for unity and excellence and would accept nothing less.

My heart pounded in my chest, and as I stopped before the altar, I found myself worrying about my appearance. Was my bun neatly tucked? Was my veil on straight? Was my robe white enough?

"Oriana. Today you enter womanhood. Today you give yourself to The Mother," the Elder said. "For it is She that gives us life and light. It is She that blesses these halls. Are you ready to give yourself to Her, sister Oriana?"

Inhaling deeply, I responded, "Yes, Elder. I am ready to give myself to The Mother. For it is She who guides my path." For months, I studied this ritual and the lines

I was to say. Over and over I repeated the vows in my head. I prayed that now, in my panic, I would not forget them. Something within me told me to get up and run. Run into the ocean, toward the white light that was on the small island that housed a portal to a realm unknown.

"Kneel, sister." The Elder's voice pulled me out of my own head, and I did as she instructed.

I looked up at her and hoped that through my veil she could not see the nervousness in my eyes. I prayed I was holding my hands so tight it would stop them from shaking.

The Elder looked up at my sisters who sat to my back. "Sister Oriana has been at this sanctuary since she was a young babe. All of you should take a lesson from her. She has walked with The Mother longer than most, today will only make it official." She looked down at me. "Recite the vows, sister Oriana."

Swallowing hard and lowering my head, I made my vows to The Mother, and with each one, I felt my freedom slipping away.

Modesty, to live humbly with no attachment to goods. Chastity, to love The Mother above all others. Obedience, to follow Her will.

With these vows, I swear to live by The Mother and allow Her to guide my life as she sees fit.

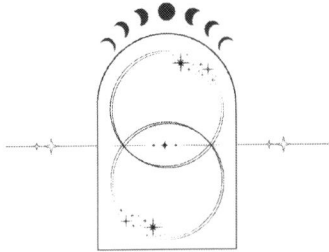

One

We had three days until the King of Elswyth arrived and forced another one of us through the portal to unknown lands. This would be the fifth year he sacrificed us to the fae realm. There were now only three sisters left in the age group he was sending, and unfortunately, I was one of those girls. Despite our pleas, the king refused to tell us why one of the sisters of this sanctuary born twenty-five years ago needed to go through the portal.

When the King first demanded us to offer ourselves as sacrifice, our Elder placed all of us in a room together. Each year, we gained more and more space as our numbers dwindled.

Cassandra and Larisa were able to find sleep. I could not. I tossed and turned in bed, begging for sleep to take me. However, the anxiety of the selection results filled my mind. What if it was me who was selected next? What if I was forced to travel through realms? What would I find beyond the portal?

I was certain it was death.

My sisters believed it was The Mother's will that sent our four sisters into the fae realm, and whoever was chosen next would be Mother blessed.

I spent my whole life devoted to The Mother at this sanctuary. Many of my sisters joined later in life, and I was the only one raised in the sanctuary from infancy. According to the elders, one day I appeared on the front steps, with no indication of who dropped me off. The only thing I was left with was a blanket with my name embroidered in the corner and a white pendant necklace, which I wear every day. Without it, anxiety filled me more than normal. Slowly, I rubbed my finger across the smooth face of the white oval stone.

Getting out of bed, I silently walked over to the balcony door and exited the room. The bright light of the full moon reflected on the sea, and the waves crashed onto the rocks down below. Closing my eyes, I took in the scent of the salty air. Trying to find my peace, I prayed to The Mother, begging Her for answers about why this was happening for the fifth year in a row.

Would there be an end before there were none of us left?

Opening my eyes, I looked to the west, to the small town of Varia. Not a single light was on, as everyone was likely settled into their beds. Our island was off the northeast coast of the continent of Elswyth. It was a crescent shape and wrapped around a smaller island. My gaze traveled over to the small island, and to the white light that shone from it. The portal to Aeros called my name. On the wind, soft voices called for me. It had for as long as I could remember, but each year it was not I who was chosen to travel through.

Reaching up, I held tight onto my pendant, and the whispers on the wind silenced. I let out a sigh of relief as the voices quieted. When I turned eighteen and took my vows, I swore that I would give up my longing for adventure. Returning to my bed, I sat up and stared at my sisters for a long moment.

Three more days until our lives changed forever.

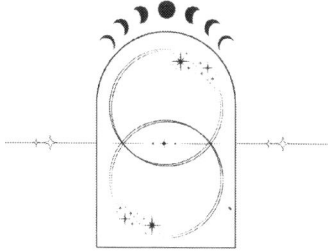

Two

Sat in a wooden pew with my head bowed, I listened to the Elder speak about the will of The Mother. How we are not to question it. How the Mother knew best. And, how everything happened for a reason. I closed my eyes as I took in her words. She gave this same sermon last year, just before the selection. During the first selection, many sisters were up in arms that the Elder allowed a man to come in and take one of us.

What was she to do? How do you say no to the King?

Little was known about the King. He isolated himself in his palace in the capital city. The only thing I knew about him was that he hated magic. He outlawed it and cut off relations to the continent to the east. It was a land full of vampires and fae, from what I understood, but there was not much literature about those lands. When the King made magic illegal, he demanded all books on magic and magical creatures destroyed.

This made the selection much more concerning. For a man who hated magic and the fae so much, why would he force us to travel to the fae realm beyond the portal? Before the selection, we all avoided the portal. Everyone in Elswyth knew of the poor village of Pendril and of the nightmarish creatures that came out of the portal just south of that small town. The people of Varia were terrified we would fall to the same fate if we approached the portal. We knew nothing about what was beyond it until the King showed up that fateful day and declared Serena would enter the portal and travel to the fae realm of Aeros. Her cries still haunted my dreams. As did my other sisters, who were lost to the portal.

"Oriana," the Elder's voice rang in my ear, and I felt a gentle hand on my shoulder.

Opening my eyes and lifting my gaze, I was surprised to see only the Elder and myself remained in the church. She offered me a smile that did not reach her eyes and sat next to me.

"The service has been over for about fifteen minutes. Want to talk about what weighs so heavy on your soul?"

I hesitated before I answered. This woman was like a mother to me. She had raised me to be the perfect acolyte of The Mother. I knew if I told her my fear about the selection, she would be disappointed in me. She, like my sisters, believed it to be The Mother's will.

"I cannot lie, Elder. I am nervous about the selection. I cannot quiet my inner fears about who we will lose next. And, if it is me, what waits for me in the realm beyond?"

"Oh, child," she sighed and shook her head. Even as she lowered her head, her perfect white bun did not move an inch. The Elder was perfect in every way. I struggled to keep my long blonde hair in a bun. Once during a ritual, my bun had fallen loose. The look of disappointment in her eyes mirrored how she looked at that moment. "If it is The Mother's will, you will go. And she will protect you in what lies ahead. The Mother does not give more than you can handle. Out of anyone, you should understand this. You have lived under The Mother's guidance your whole life. Listen to what she tells you, and you won't make a wrong choice." She stood and walked to the aisle, turning to me and offering a nod before leaving the church.

I sat there for another half hour, in silence.

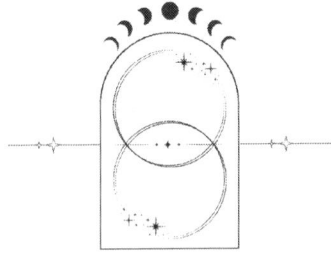

Three

Today was the day the King was going to arrive. According to the Elder, it needed to be us three that greeted him. Never in previous years had we done this. Before, the Elder met with the king in private. She would then come and tell us which of us he selected to travel to Elswyth for an undisclosed task.

This would be the first time I would lay my eyes on the king.

The Elder, Cassandra, Larisa, and I all walked down the street in a single-file line to the docks. It was very rare this many of us would travel in town together. Normally, we always traveled in pairs. I kept my eyes down on the cobblestone, avoiding the gaze of the townsfolk who always gawked at us as if we were some oddity. I suppose we were in our long white robes and veils that covered our faces. Even in the heat of summer, we wore our robes. Luckily, in the warmer months, our veils were made of a thin, breathable material.

It had been many months since I left the sanctuary. The crowds always put me at unease. However, in the back of my mind, I could not help but regret I spent so much time shut away. What if I was selected and my end was near? There was so much in life I missed out on, so many sights unseen. My entire life had been wasted hiding away on this tiny island.

The last time I had been to town was to gather supplies from the general store. I met a woman who traveled here from the capital city. She was convinced there was someone in town who had magic. Apparently, it was some long-lost cousin of hers from her mother's side. I often wondered what happened to her. I believe her name was Stephanie. I prayed no one reported her for speaking of magic. There are people in this town who would report people for discussing magic to gain a reward from it. She was a kind girl, but very confused. As no one in Varia — or in all of Elswyth — had magic. Were people from the capitol that brazen to go against their king's order that they would actively search magic users, and admit themselves to be one?

When we arrived at the dock, I was in awe of the massive ship that belonged to the king. On the sail was printed the royal crest. The symbol of the royal family never made sense to me. It was made of four squares of two different patterns. The first was a pattern of red and white diamonds that was on the first and fourth quarter, and the second was a black and yellow oddly shaped cross. According to history, these were the two coats of arms from the first families that founded Elswyth centuries ago.

A tall and skinny man in a suit far too nice to be a dock worker approached us. He offered a small bow and looked up at the Elder. "Excuse me, you must be the Elder of the sanctuary. May we speak in private before the king disembarks?"

"Of course," she responded. Her gaze then slowly fell to us. "Girls, stay here," she said before walking off with the man.

Cassandra took my hand and squeezed it tight. I looked over to her and saw the worry in her eyes. Larisa walked closer to us, and the three of us formed a tight circle.

"What is wrong?" I asked in a whisper.

"I wasn't nervous until I saw the ship. This is really happening again, isn't it?" Cassandra's voice quivered as she spoke.

"Cas, this isn't like you," Larisa responded. "I have never seen you this nervous about anything." She leaned in closer and drew her eyebrows together.

Cas took in a deep breath before she spoke. "What if Ori is right? What if beyond the portal is nothing but a cold and lonely death?" She pulled her hands to her chest and wrung them together.

Larisa shot me a glare. "Ori doesn't know what she's talking about. I am sure the others are over there having the best time of their lives. Maybe they all got married to fae nobility."

"Fae nobility," Casandra scoffed. "No such thing. I never told anyone this, but the town where I am from, Pendril, has a portal there, too. The fae that travel through that portal are blood-thirsty beasts! Savages! Monsters!" Casandra got louder with every word.

Glancing up after catching movement in my peripheral vision, I noticed more townsfolk looking at us. Taking Casandra's hands, I held them tight. "Will you lower your voice? Everyone is starting to stare at us. We do not want to displease the Elder."

Casandra let out a deep sigh. "I'm sorry," she now spoke in a softer tone. "If I am chosen, I am not sure if I have the strength."

"The Mother only gives us what we can handle." I mimicked the words of the Elder, hoping they would bring comfort to my sister. It was nice to think that way, though I wasn't sure if I believed it.

Before anyone could say anything else, the Elder approached us. "Come along, ladies. It seems the King is a bit seasick from his travels. He will meet us tonight in the sanctuary for dinner and explain everything to you then."

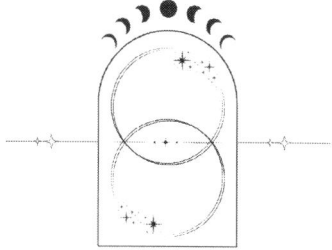

Four

My sisters and I returned to our room as soon as we got back to the sanctuary. We only had a few moments to rest before we had to complete our duties before the king's arrival. The first thing I did was remove my veil.

"Ori, your bun is a wreck," Cas laughed.

"It's this humidity! Nothing I do keeps it nice." I tried to slick down the flyaways with my hands but was without success.

"Come sit." She motioned to the vanity stool. "I will fix it."

"You're Mother sent. You know that?" I smiled up at her as I sat.

"Hey! What about me?" Larisa teased. She rushed over and sat in the chair next to the vanity against the wall.

"You both are!" I watched in the mirror as Cas let down my bun and ran her fingers through my ashy blond hair. I looked very different from the rest of my sisters. While most of them had tan skin, like most people from the island, I had very fair skin. While their eyes were brown or green, mine were a dark blue like the raging sea. I was also the only one with ashy blonde hair.

Cas fixed my hair into the most perfect bun I had ever seen. "There you go." She walked over and sat on the edge of her bed. "No matter what happens, I want you all to know I love you all." Tears misted her dark brown eyes.

Larisa and I rushed over to her, sitting on either side and wrapped her in a tight hug.

"No matter what, we will all meet again someday," Larisa said softly.

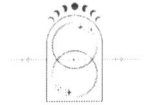

THE SACRIFICE OF AEROS

The Elder had her private dining room set up for a feast. We spent all afternoon preparing the meal for our king. This was the first time he would dine with us at the sanctuary. Never had I made a meal for someone so important. I believed I was a good cook, but tonight would put my skills to the test. It would also show if my sisters were being kind, or if I really could cook. We had just finished setting the table when one of our other sisters rushed into the room.

"The King is here! The Elder is coming up with him now. She said everything must be done within the next two minutes." Ellie said in between breaths.

"Well, luckily everything is ready for him," I said with a smile.

"Shoo. You don't want to be caught up in the mess we have found ourselves in," Cas said.

Ellie was five years younger than us. I was always so envious of the women who lived here who were not within our age range. How I wished and prayed we could live as carefree as they did. She left us, and the three of us stood at the door, awaiting the King's arrival. It was not long after that we could hear the Elder's voice and one of an older man. When the door opened, my sisters and I all fell into a curtsy.

"Please stand," the man chuckled.

We did. My heart skipped a beat as my eyes fell on the King. A top of his ash-blonde hair sat a crown of white stones that matched my pendant. When I stared into his dark blue eyes, it was almost like staring into my own. I wished we had worn our veils tonight so I could hide the shocked look on my face.

The King's eyes also went wide as he looked at me. I swore I saw a silver mist in them. "It really is you." His voice cracked as he spoke. "I did not want it to be you."

"What... What's going on?" Casandra asked.

"Why don't we all sit for this conversation?" The Elder said, walking more into the room. She pulled out the chair at the head of the table. "Please, my king, sit here. Oriana, please sit next to him." The Elder then assigned seats to my other sisters. Two royal guards stood in the doorway as we all sat. The king never once removed his eyes from me, and I was unable to look away from him, either.

Once everyone was sat, the words spilled from the King's lips. "Many years ago, when I first became king, I met a very beautiful woman. She worked in the castle as a sorceress. Her name was Ariana."

I was shocked to hear a sorceress had worked within a castle. What shocked me even more was how close her name was to my own.

The king continued. "She was the most beautiful woman I had ever laid my eyes on, but I was already sworn to another. A noble girl who would strengthen my line. That woman is now my wife and the Queen of Elswyth. But I still could not stop thinking of the sorceress who had stolen my heart."

My sisters and I all listened closely to the king as he told his tale. My heart pounded in my chest.

"I was a weak man and allowed the sorceress into my bed, time and time again, behind the queen's back. It was not long before she came to me and told me she was with child. My first child, a child I was not supposed to have." He took a deep breath. "During that time, the vampire king to the east threatened our land. He had been sending letters, telling me this land was his, and soon we would all be his chattel. I did not know where to turn, so I prayed to The Mother. I could not allow my land to be turned into a farm for vampires. Ariana worked hard, trying to find us a solution against the vampire king. She sent out a call to the fae realms. That call was answered when the fae king of Aeros wrote to me, claiming he could help keep away the vampires. In exchange, he wanted my magical child, and that on her twentieth birthday, she would be wed to his son. I agreed."

My breath quickened as I listened to the king. I focused on his fair skin, his ashy hair, and his blue eyes that mirrored mine.

No, this cannot be.

The king continued speaking. "I had no intention of letting him take my daughter. I tried to hide Ariana and my child from him, but when she gave birth, Ariana lost her life. I could not bring an illegitimate child into the palace and inform my wife of my affair. Instead, I did what needed to be done. I outlawed magic. I gave my baby a pendant that belonged to her mother and named her after her mother, so she would always have a piece of her true family. With no other choice, I sent her to the one place I thought The Mother would protect her and bound her magic to keep it hidden." He paused for a moment, looking at me. "On her twentieth year, her betrothed wrote to me, claiming it was time to pay up. I sent a random girl into the portal, but she did not make it. She could not handle the passing. I learned too late that the king placed a curse on the portal. Any who passed that did not have magic in their blood would die."

A sob ripped from Casandra and Larisa's throats, and my hand rose to cover my mouth and muffle my own reaction.

"I didn't mean to kill those poor girls. I did not know." He turned to look at me. "I simply wanted to protect you. My only daughter. But now the King of Aeros is coming to take you, and there is nothing I can do to stop him."

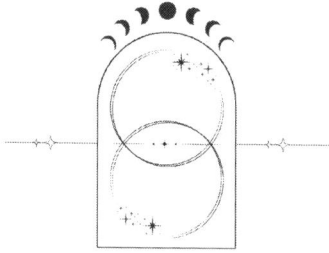

Five

No. This couldn't be true.

Ringing filled my ears, and I felt my stomach turn. This was all too much. I could not handle the reality that was being forced upon me. This all had to be a dream of some sort. The room filled with the sounds of Larisa's and Casandra's sobs. When I looked over to the Elder, her face was cold as stone and her gaze was set on the King.

I stood up from the table and rushed out of the dining room. I could not face the man I now knew to be my father. My whole life I wondered what happened to my parents, wondered why they would abandon me.

It was so hard to love yourself when the people who were supposed to love you didn't love you enough to keep you. I struggled with that my entire life. To learn my father was the king, my mother was a woman he had an affair with, and that he threw me away as if I never meant anything to him tore my soul to shreds.

I marched my way out of the sanctuary, ignoring everyone I passed on my way out. Tears streamed down my face as I made my way to the rocky cliffside. Waves crashed against it as I stood there for a while, staring at the white light off in the distance. I heard my name whispered in the wind, calling me to it. Rage boiled inside me at the sound. My sisters were dead. That white light was a reminder of everything wrong in my life.

What waited for me across the portal was a fae male who was to be my bridegroom. A man I had never met. I vowed myself to The Mother. Never once did I ever think about breaking those vows. Some of the other sisters may have blurred the line, but never me. I understood the role of a wife, and I refused to be that for this male. For *any* male.

My hand reached up to grab my pendant. Over the last twenty-five years, I had used it to find comfort, but for the first time, it made my stomach turn. I ripped it off my neck and threw it into the ocean, letting out a scream. A bright white flashed from the portal, nearly blinding me.

I screamed and screamed, long after the necklace fell into the dark water.

"Those are some lungs you have." A deep voice came from behind me.

I nearly jumped out of my own skin. There were no men who lived at the sanctuary, and this was not one of the voices I recognized from the King's men. I spun and saw a very handsome man. Never had I seen anyone so tall and muscular in the village. He must have come with the king. He had his hands tucked into the pockets of his dark jeans, and his white ink tattoos of geometric shapes popped against his dark skin. He looked down at me with a concerned expression.

"You scared me!" I said, held my hand to my chest, and took in a deep breath.

"Well, I guess we are even. When I heard your screams, I thought you were being murdered. Glad to see you're not." He took a step closer to me.

I bit my lip as I met his gaze. For the first time in my life, I found myself enthralled by a man. The bright white light of the portal reflected in his chocolate brown eyes. Something deep within me was calling for this man, and I found myself hating my chastity vow. Quickly, I pushed down those desires. "What are you doing here? I don't recognize you from the village. Are you here with the king?"

The man offered a chuckle. "You can say that. Tell me, why were you screaming out at the sea?"

I stared at him for a long moment, narrowing my eyes. I wasn't exactly sure about how I felt about this man. "Quite nosy, aren't you?"

"I'd like to think of it as inquisitive." He smirked.

"There you are!" I heard the king's voice off in the distance.

Turning toward the king, I watched as he and the Elder quickly approached us. Fear grew in the king's eyes as he got closer to and looked up at the mystery man.

"You said I could have one more day!" The king shouted.

"You promised her to me five years ago, human," the mystery man said in an aggressive tone. "I could not trust your words. Not after four women died due to your deceit. My father may have continuously allowed you to try to snake your way out of the deal, but now that I am king, you won't be so lucky." He took a step toward the king.

My eyes widened as I realized who stood before me and fear froze me in place. Even though my mind screamed for me to run, to jump into the ocean to escape, my body would not comply. My betrothed turned his head to look down at me and winked. His true form was revealed to me as he grew to seven feet, his ears became pointed, and white feathered wings unfurled from his back.

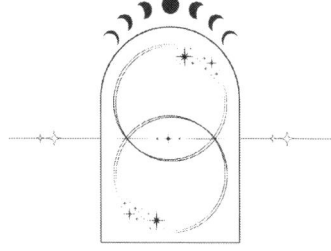

Six

My heart pounded in terror as the world around me spun. This had to be a nightmare, as I did not want to accept this as my reality. I looked over to see the Elder had fainted and collapsed. The King rushed to her side, trying to wake her. My betrothed had his hard stare set on me, and it burned into my skin.

Staggering back from the fae male to gain distance from him, I screamed, " I will not go with you! I will not marry you." The calling that I had toward this man still pulled on my heart, but I could not allow that feeling to win. I would be no one's bride.

The male let out a deep chuckle, and a heavy weight pressed down onto my body.

Falling to my knees, I looked up at him and snarled. He stepped forward, closed the gap between us, and knelt before me. Gripping my chin, he forced me to stare directly into his rich brown eyes. "You have no choice. A contract was signed. If broken, the deal my father had with yours would be undone. Tell me, do you want your land to be conquered by vampires? Would you rather be a vampire's pet than my wife? At least I won't feed from you. Take from you what gives you life. All I ask is for your loyalty and cooperation. Magic for magic. A favor for a favor." His voice was like rich velvet.

My stomach turned as he spoke. There was no choice here. It was time I accepted the fate The Mother planned for me, no matter how much I hated it. Frustration filled me, tears misted my eyes, and I tried to hold them back. I could not let him see me falter. "If I come with you, will you still protect this land from the vampires?" I asked softly, but not weakly.

"Of course. Fae are bound by their word." He shot the King of Elswyth a pointed glare. "We do not try to trick our way out of bargains made." He lowered his gaze back to mine. "Do we have a deal, darling?"

"We have a deal," I said in defeat.

A smirk grew on his face, and the weight I felt on my body lifted. "Come along." He reached his hand down to me. I took it, and he assisted me up. The fae male looked back over to my father. "Be lucky we are not the fae of Irolyth. For if you tried to swindle your way out of the deal you made, it would have been *you* that died, and not innocent women." He picked me up, cradling me in his arms. "Hold on tight, darling. Flying can be a bit scary for first-timers."

"Let me go! I need to say goodbye to my sisters!" I squirmed in his grasp.

"We have wasted too much time already. Maybe you will see them again when the task I need you to complete is done." With that, he flapped his wings and launched us into the sky.

I wrapped my arms around his neck, clinging to him. Shutting my eyes tight, my body trembled against the solid muscle of his chest. "I'm going to fall!" I cried out.

"No, you aren't. I would never drop a pretty little thing like you."

After what seemed like an eternity, I felt the fae's feet hit solid ground. Relief washed over me. Only then did I open my eyes. White light nearly blinded me as I did. When my vision adjusted, I realized we stood directly in front of the portal. My heart pounded harder in my chest.

"No need to be scared. I've got you, darling," he said softly.

"What if I die, too?" My voice quivered as I spoke. My thoughts raced with the fear I would meet the same fate as my sisters. What if no mortal was met to pass through into the fae realm?

"You won't. You were born for this." He offered me a soft smile that did not meet his eyes. That expression offered me no comfort.

Before I could answer, the man stepped through the portal, pulling me with him, and a flash of white filled my vision.

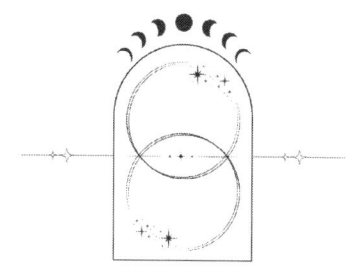

Seven

Everything came back into focus, and we were now standing in a small grassy field. The sun was shining, and it warmed my skin. The fae male gently set me down on my feet. I turned to face him, and the glow of the portal haloed him, making him look like a god.

I turned away and then realized where exactly we were. The small grassland we stood in was an island, but beyond the land was not a sea, it was clouds. I took a few steps forward and looked beyond. Three more islands floated in the sky. The underneath of the islands were rough and jagged as if they had been ripped from the ground. One had large oak trees, another a massive city, and the farthest one had a castle.

"Welcome to Aeros, darling. Be mindful not to get too close to the edge. I wouldn't want you to fall to your death before your usefulness wore out."

I spun my head and shot him a pointed glare. "I am plenty useful! I do not need a man to tell me what I am worth or not worth."

He let out a chuckle. "Feisty. Good, I like that. Keep that up. You will need it for what lies ahead."

"What exactly is that?" I raised my eyebrow at him.

"All in good time. Come along. Let's get back to the castle so I can take you to your room." Stepping toward me, he lifted me into his arms holding me close. He launched into the air once again.

This time, I forced myself to keep my eyes wide open. I wanted to take in everything I could about the new realm I found myself in. The island with the trees was the first we flew over. Half of it was a forest, the other half was farmland. Winged fae waved up at us as we flew overhead. Other than the wings and pointed ears, the ones below us almost looked normal. They looked human.

Would they act human? Or, would the fae be brutal beasts?

The next island was a large city. It resembled images of the capital city of Elswyth I had seen, with towering buildings and bustling streets. If the inhabitants were not fae, I would have thought this to be a fairly normal place. Just as we passed the city, another fae male flew up next to us. My entire body tensed as he came into view. He had similar white tattoos to my bridegroom. They stood out against his tan skin.

I wondered what they meant.

"My King, you have returned!" He cheered as he flew by our side.

"Indeed. Glad to hear your senses are still intact, Artemis," my betrothed responded in a sarcastic tone.

"You are such an ass," he laughed. "I see the human king did not try to escape his deal again. Hello, little one."

I tried to speak, but words did not escape my throat. Being in the air made me uneasy, and all I wanted was to be on the ground.

"Again, such a great observation. Maybe notice the girl is afraid, and that this may not be the best time for introductions?"

The other man flew ahead and looked back at us. Cocking his head, he shrugged. "Well, I am already here. Hello, human. I am Artemis. Captain of the Guard and King Malachi's best friend. It is a pleasure to finally meet you!"

Ah, so my betrothed's name was finally revealed. Honestly, I thought his name would be something much more.... Mystical? Something in a tongue I was not familiar with. I did not expect the fae to have names like Malachi or Artemis. Maybe they were more like the people of Elswyth than I believed.

Malachi let out a low growl. "Art, I have one nerve left, and you are getting on it. Shoo!" He flapped his wings hard, forcing us to fly faster and to pass Artemis.

"That nerve has my name seared into it. It is mine to be on as much as I see fit!" Artemis caught up to us and flashed a bright smile.

Malachi rolled his eyes but said nothing in response. A moment later, he was planting his feet onto the ground in front of the castle, and Artemis landed next to us. Gently, Malachi put me down, and I stumbled a bit as I found my footing.

Artemis rushed over to me, took my hand in his, and brought it to his lips. They gently brushed against my skin. "Welcome home, little one. Glad I'm finally meeting you after all these years. What is your name?"

My eyes widened, and a blush took over my cheeks. I stuttered as I stared into his emerald eyes. Now that I was firmly on the ground, I could speak my name. "Oriana."

Malachi forced himself in between the two of us. "Artemis. This is my soon-to-be wife. Please don't try to charm her like you do every other woman you meet."

A smirk crossed his face. "Well, don't you have your serious pants on today." He huffed. "We have shared before. I'm sure she wouldn't mind. Would you, little one?"

"Yes, I do mind! I am not a toy to be shared!" I glared at him.

"Oh, you misunderstand me. Not a toy, a treasure." He offered me a wink and a predatory smirk.

"Artemis, fuck off before I send you below. Don't you have something to do?" Malachi crossed his arms and glared down at his friend. Artemis was tall, but Malachi was a few inches taller.

"I suppose I do." He gave a nonchalant shrug. "Nice meeting you, little one. Hopefully, we will meet again soon." With a strong flap of his wings, he launched into the air, leaving dust in his wake.

Malachi watched until Artemis was a good distance away. "I am sorry about him. Ignore him. He is a thorn in my side." He turned to look at me. "Shall I give you a tour of the castle and then take you to your chambers to rest?"

"That sounds great, actually."

"Wonderful. I will allow you a few days to adjust to the time here, as we are on an opposite day-night cycle compared to Elswyth. Once adjusted, I will teach you how to use your magic." He gave me an up-and-down glance. "I understand that I pulled you away from dinner. You must be starving."

I wanted to deny him, but the growling of my stomach couldn't. I had been so busy all day preparing for the king's visit that I barely had time to feed myself. "Do you have food a human could eat?"

Malachi threw his head back and laughed. "We eat the same things. Come along. I will take you to my private dining room after the tour."

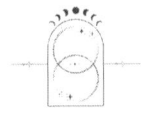

The castle was very beautiful. Never in my life had I been anywhere so opulent. It was full of gorgeous white marble floors and pillars, courtyards filled with colorful flowers in full bloom, and a massive library. Never had I seen so many books in one place. Often in the sanctuary, I would find myself in the library, but that was just a small room with about five shelves. The library here was beyond my imagination. It was seven stories tall, and not a single shelf was left unfilled.

At the end of the tour, Malachi led me to his private dining room. It was a cozy space with a fireplace on one wall. On either side of the fireplace hung two black tapestries that had similar markings to my bridegroom's tattoos. Malachi pulled out my seat, allowed me to sit, and then gently pushed me closer to the table. He then took his seat at the head of the dark mahogany table.

As soon as we sat, one of his servants brought out a roasted pheasant on a silver platter and placed it in the center of the table. Another servant had an entire cart full of sides.

"Would you like light or dark meat?" The servant asked as he carved up the bird.

"Light, please," I offered a smile. It was so odd to have someone wait on me, back at the sanctuary it was required that we were self-reliant.

"Ah yes, the breast is my favorite as well." A familiar voice teased from behind me.

Malachi's gaze shot in that direction. "Artemis, you were not invited to this lunch. Leave."

"What kind of guard captain would I be if I allowed my king to be alone with some strange human girl? Besides, I am hungry." Artemis walked to the other side of the table and leaned over it. Taking my hand in his, he gently placed a kiss on my knuckles. "Lovely to see you again, little one," he said with a wink.

Malachi let out a low growl. "Sit. Eat. Be quiet."

Releasing my hand, Artemis rolled his eyes as he took his seat. "What a benevolent king. So, tell me, Oriana, what do you think of Aeros so far?"

"It's beautiful. Never did I expect to see islands floating in the sky. The castle is wonderful as well. Back home, I lived on a small island. We had nothing like this." Everything in this castle broke my vow of modesty. It was lavish and flashy. I prayed that The Mother would not resent me for being here in such luxury.

Artemis leaned forward. "Oh, I would love to fly you around the islands and give you a tour of the city."

"Enough!" Malachi slammed his fist on the table and the dishes clattered. "Stop flirting with my betrothed. She has gone through enough today."

"Just for today?" Artemis smirked.

Malachi picked up his table knife and threw it toward Artemis, who quickly dodged out of the way. The knife stuck into the wall behind Artemis. "Hm. What a shame. Next time, I won't miss, but since you live, you can stay for lunch." Malachi offered Artemis a genuine smile and looked toward the servant who finished carving the bird. "Torin, please bring out a third plate for Art."

"Awe, see. I knew you wanted me here!" Artemis laughed.

Torin left and quickly returned with a plate. Once Artemis' place was set, Torin served us some of the carved pheasant. He placed a slice of breast meat onto my plate first before attending to the men. The other servant came to my side and offered a small bow.

"Good afternoon, my lady. I have some sides for you to choose from." She listed all the options on her cart.

There were way too many to pick from. Many looked familiar to me, but some were unrecognizable and exotic. After a moment, I decided on the sweet potatoes with pecans and the garlic butter green beans. "Please enjoy," she said before moving on to the king.

I took a bite of the meat first, and it melted in my mouth. The taste of rosemary and sage exploded on my tongue. The sweet potatoes were fluffy and delightful, and the garlic butter on the beans was one of the most delicious sauces I ever had.

While I ate, Malachi and Artemis bickered back and forth about everything. The two seemed more like brothers than king and guard captain. I could not help but wonder how close they were, especially after Artemis commented on them sharing women in the past.

"I cannot tell if you guys enjoy each other's company or not," I said in a moment of silence.

"We are best friends," Artemis answered. "No matter what King Grump says."

Malachi rolled his eyes. "I am not grumpy. Will you stop? Yes, Artemis and I have been friends since we were boys. He was assigned as my personal guard when we were ten, and when I became king, I made him captain."

"It has been an honor to serve by your side and constantly piss you off for the last thirty years," Artemis said as he took a big bite of meat.

"A thorn in my side until the very end." Malachi offered a genuine smile.

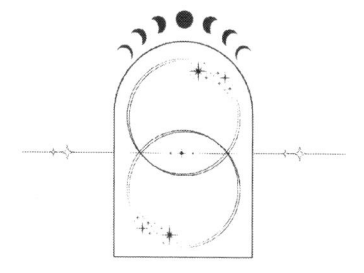

Eight

Three days passed, and I still was struggling to adjust to the day and night cycle of the fae realm. It was the complete opposite of my old schedule. Even though it was day here in Aeros, it was the middle of the night in Elswyth. My anxiety also made it hard for me to fall asleep, so I would not find rest until the early hours of their morning, and woke up just after lunchtime. It was not a sleep schedule I would recommend to anyone.

During those three days, my soon-to-be husband was nowhere to be found, and neither was his guard captain. However, I was provided with a lady's maid named Violet. She looked very different from the other fae I had seen here. While she had wings like the others, they were orange with a white border and delicate, almost like butterflies. Most of the fae of Aeros had darker hair, her fiery red hair was cut into a short, pointed bob. She was very kind and always made sure I had a meal waiting for me when I awoke. She also made sure to keep my bathing chamber stocked with luxurious soaps and perfumes.

Rolling over in bed, I stared out the window and stared out into the clouds. My room was in a tower of the castle that gave me a great view of the sky and the three other islands. There was a soft knock at the door, and it caused me to sit up.

"Who is it?" I called out.

"It's me, my lady," Violet called out from beyond the door.

"Come in," I responded.

She walked in with a small pile of folded clothes in her hands. "Good afternoon. The King has requested your audience."

"And if I refuse to see him?" I questioned.

"No one refuses King Malachi." She narrowed her eyes at me and put the clothes on the bed next to me. "This is what you will wear to meet with him."

I picked up the clothes and examined them. "I have never worn pants before. Can't I wear one of my dresses?" At the sanctuary, it was forbidden to wear pants. It was not ladylike and was not The Mother's will. Some of the sisters who joined later in life told stories of what pants felt like when wearing them. Honestly, I saw no issue in others wearing them, but too much had changed for me over the last three days. I could not stand the thought of anything else changing.

"A dress would not be suitable for what he has planned for you. Today, you will start exploring your magic! How exciting!" A smile grew across her face.

Not exciting at all. Ever since I learned I came from a line of sorceresses, the thought of my magic was at the forefront of my mind. What type of magic was I capable of, and why did the fae king need it so badly that he would make a deal for my hand in marriage to his son? "Give me about five minutes, and I will be ready to go see the king."

"Please let me know if there is anything you need. I will be waiting just outside." She curtsied and exited the room. The very first day we met, she tried to help me undress. That was terribly awkward. I informed her I had no issue dressing myself, and for her to wait outside until I was ready.

I stripped from my night dress and put on the tight leather pants. Looking across the room, I examined myself in the full-length mirror, my focus traveling down my curves. Never had I worn something so form-fitting. As I put on my top, I prayed to The Mother that Artemis would not be there as well. Based on how flirty he was,

I was not sure if he could handle seeing me in these pants. Or, how I would handle his reactions.

Once I was dressed, I braided my long blonde hair and allowed it to fall down the center of my back. Taking one more look in the mirror, I did not recognize the woman who looked back at me. A few days ago, I was an orphan and a devout follower of The Mother. Now, I was an illegitimate princess betrothed to a king and a fledgling sorceress.

Pulling my gaze away from myself, I sighed deeply.

Joining Violet in the hall, she offered me another warm smile. "You look wonderful! Just as expected. Come along, we wouldn't want to keep the Kking waiting any longer." She turned and walked down the hall toward the stairs that led down the tower. I was not a prisoner of the tower, but after the initial tour, I found myself rarely leaving. Violet led me outside to a training ring behind the castle. The plush grass gave way to rocks and sand.

Malachi sat on one of the large stones across the grounds. His stare burned through me as his attention focused directly on me. "Thank you, Violet. Leave us."

"Yes, my King." She bowed and quickly flew off.

The fae king slowly rose from his rock and made his way toward me. "What a shame," he sighed.

"What?" I raised my eyebrow in response.

Malachi continued to walk in my direction as he spoke. "It is a shame what your father turned you into. That he locked away your magic and kept you from being who you truly are. I was hoping by the time we wed, you would be a powerful sorceress. No worries. I have taught many fae children how to control the magic of Aeros. I do not imagine it would be much harder teaching you." He stopped directly in front of me and offered me a comforting smile.

"The magic of Aeros?" This place was so strange. From the floating islands to the white tattoos. It was hard to accept that this wasn't some odd dream.

"Yes, we here practice gravitational magic. Thank The Mother for it. My great-grandfather would not have been able to save our people from The Great Calamity without his powerful magic." With a rise of his palm, a large rock on the outside of the training circle rose into the air about three feet. When he dropped his hand, the stone crashed back to the ground.

I stared at the rock in shock. It was the first time I had seen magic. I wondered if this was what I could do as well. I spun my head back to Malachi. "The Great Calamity?" I raised my eyebrow.

"You really know nothing of Aeros, do you?"

"Nothing at all." I hated I was in a place I knew nothing about. It made me feel helpless.

"Come sit." He turned and pointed to the smaller rock that was next to the one he went to sit on.

Walking over, I sat down on the warm stone, looking up at him. He looked down at me with a smile that did not reach his deep brown eyes, inhaling deeply before he spoke. "Many centuries ago, Aeros was below the clouds. There was a great calamity that occurred that ruined the land and destroyed the kingdom. My great-grandfather raised the capital city, the castle, and the surrounding lands into the sky to save our people. We have tried several times to go below the clouds to see what is happening down there, but all who go, never return. There is a prophecy that has been passed down by our people that a daughter of a sorceress with sapphires for eyes will save us, and return us to the land below."

"What was the calamity?" I asked.

"No one here knows. My great-grandfather did not make it into the sky. And anyone who was around before the rising never spoke of it. I was hoping you would be able to shed some light on what had happened. But, seeing you never even knew your mother, I doubt you will be much help."

I wanted to be angry at that statement, but he was right. How was I going to be able to help? I knew nothing of this world. I barely knew about my world. How was I supposed to save them from this calamity? "I am sorry, but you know I cannot help you. Why not return me home?"

"Because I have not given up on you. Your father may have cut your worth into a nobody human destined to live a life hidden away, but I know you can be so much more." He stood. "First, we will see how much of your magic you can feel. We will start there and then progress to see what you can do with it. Stand." He turned toward me, offering me a hand up.

I took it and stood. How could someone who just met me have so much confidence in me?

"Close your eyes, darling." I did as he instructed. "Breathe slowly. In. Out. In. Out. Find your inner peace deep within yourself." I felt him release my hand.

For a moment, there was silence as I took in my deep breaths. I searched for that inner peace he wanted me to find. It seemed as if nothing was working. I was just standing there, breathing, and feeling the sun beat down on me.

"Darling, you got this. Focus harder. Search for the light inside yourself. For your core. Your essence." His voice was calm and soothing. It sounded as if he was directly behind me.

Focusing harder, I was finally able to see a soft, glowing light in the distance. It flickered and struggled to stay lit, but it was there, and fighting.

No, it was me that was fighting. I was fighting to keep the light on. Fighting to pull power forward and to claim it as my own.

Before I could focus enough to gain control, the ground trembled, causing me to lose my balance and fall. Malachi caught me in his arms before I hit the ground. I looked up at him with worry as the quake stopped.

"Never in my forty years has there been an earthquake on the islands." His voice shook as he spoke. He helped me stand. I held tight to his muscular arms as I regained my balance.

A short moment later, Artemis landed beside us.

"Sir, half of island three has fallen."

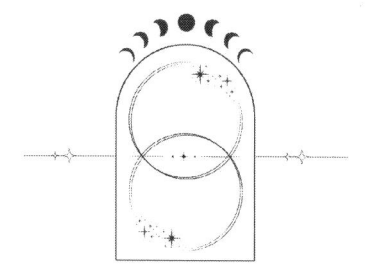

Nine

Two days had passed since the falling. Malachi sent me back into the castle after Artemis had shown up in the training yard, and I had not seen him since. According to Violet, never had any of the islands fallen below the clouds. Some part of me couldn't help but wonder if it was my fault. Did my magic cause the quake? Maybe the prophecy was about me causing the collapse of Aeros, instead of bringing it safely to the ground.

Even with everything that had happened, I was able to get more adjusted to my new sleep cycle. For the first time, I was able to get restful sleep and was awoken by the rising sun. Looking out the window, I could not help but admire the golden hue that was cascaded across the clouds. Quick knocks rattled off the door, and it opened before I could say anything.

"The king wishes to have breakfast with you!" Violet squealed with excitement as she skipped toward me with a teal dress in hand. "Quickly get dressed! We do not want to keep him waiting." She handed the dress to me, exited the room, then closed the door behind her.

I could not decide if I was excited to see him again or not. There was something within me that gravitated toward him, but there was something else that longed to return home and forget any of this had ever happened. I was relieved that today I was given a dress to wear. While the pants were nice, they were not something I really wanted to wear daily.

Once dressed and ready for the day, I met with Violet outside in the hall. She guided me down the tower steps, and to the King's private dining room. He was standing right outside of the entrance waiting for us.

"Thank you, Violet. You are dismissed."

She bowed to him and rushed away.

My eyes met with Malachi's, and he offered me a soft smile.

"I am sorry I have not had much time to see you these past few days. We are still working on figuring out what caused the collapse. That is no excuse. As your soon-to-be husband, I should be making time to see you. Please come in, sit, eat. I had the chefs prepare us a lovely breakfast!" He turned and entered the dining room.

"You don't think it has anything to do with me trying to connect with my magic do you?" I asked as I followed him into the dining room.

Malachi stopped. He stood there for a moment, then turned to me. "Of course not. Who said that to you? I will send them below the clouds right now." Anger flared in his deep brown eyes.

"No one! No one said that to me. I was just worried it was." I looked down and fiddled with my thumbs.

He took a step forward, closing the gap between us. Gently, he lifted my chin to force my gaze to meet his. "Darling, do not ever doubt yourself. Do not ever speak poorly about yourself. You are new to magic, yes, but in no way are you the cause of what happened. You could never be responsible for something so terrible," he said in a soft tone. "Now sit, eat." He pulled away and walked over to the table, pulling out a chair, and motioned for me to sit.

I did and my eyes went wide at the food that was laid out for us. Malachi sat next to me. "This looks wonderful!" My eyes scanned across the table at the fruit, meats, and pastries available.

"It tastes amazing. I have the best chefs in all of Aeros." He said as he piled meat onto his plate.

I made myself a small yogurt parfait with berries and almond granola and took a few pieces of extra crispy bacon.

"I hope this is all to your liking. If there is something you want that is not here, please let me know. I can have the chefs make it." He said as he took a bite of sausage.

"This is more than enough. Thank you!" Looking over the table again, I wondered what anyone could want more. Never had I seen such a wide selection of foods.

"Wonderful. Now we can discuss why I really wanted to see you this morning." His eyes narrowed as his tone got more serious.

"What is it?" I raised an eyebrow at him.

"Our wedding. It will be tonight at sundown." He said as he stuck a piece of ham into his mouth.

"I'm sorry. Our wedding?"

"Yes. You were promised to me. We will be wed, per our deal. Trust me, I am not thrilled, either, by the pace of things. I would love for us to be able to get to know each other more before we make everything official. However, it may be another key to unlocking your magic and returning us to below the clouds."

"I—I am not ready to be a wife," I stumbled on my words. Even though I knew he was my betrothed and knew I was to marry him, I was shocked it was so soon. I thought I would have time to adjust to my new life. Have time to get out of this arrangement.

"Darling, Ori." The way he purred my name pulled me from my own thoughts. Made me crave to hear it again. "I understand the lifestyle you used to live before coming here did not prepare you to be a wife. Other than in ceremony, we will go at your pace. You shall keep your private room. I will never force myself or anything upon you. I want you to feel safe and comfortable. I also do not want to rush into anything before I get to know you, your wants, your passions, and your desires. I know this is not how you imagined your life, but you have had my heart ever since our fathers made their deal. Please give me the chance to win yours."

My jaw dropped slightly as I took in his words. He bared his entire heart for me. What kind of woman would I be to not give someone a chance who showed such venerability?

To be honest, I liked this side of him. The side that was honest about his feelings. The side that was not afraid to say what was on his mind.

"I understand. We will wed tonight, and I will give you the chance you desire."

"Really?" His eyes lit up with excitement.

I nodded in response. Offering him a smile.

"I will spend every day trying to make you the happiest woman alive. You will not regret this." The smile on his face dropped, and his eyes widened. "Oh, I almost forgot!" He jumped up from his seat and dug into the pocket of his jacket. He pulled out his hand in a balled fist. "I went back and got this for you. I know you threw it away, but I could sense the immense power coming from it. I think it is something you may want to hang onto." He extended his arm toward me and opened his palm.

Inhaling deeply, I took in the sight of something that I never expected to see ever again. The white pendant necklace I'd thrown into the ocean in anger lay flat in his palm. "How did you find it?" Taking the beloved piece of jewelry from his hand, I examined it closely. It was hard to believe this was the same necklace I had my whole life. I threw it never expecting to see it again.

"To my surprise, when I returned to look for it, it washed up on the shore of the small island the portal is on back in Elswyth. It seemed it was making its way to you, whether I had gone to retrieve it or not," he let out a deep chuckle.

I thought if my necklace was gone, my problems would be as well. It was the one thing my father left me with when he abandoned me at the sanctuary. This pendant was the thing that linked me to my mother, to my magic.

At that moment, I hated it. But now, with it back in my possession, I was glad to have it.

"Will you allow me to put it on you?" Malachi asked nervously.

I gave him a nod in response. He took the necklace from my hand, walked around so he stood behind me, and placed the chain around my neck. Once the clasp locked, I felt as if, once again, I was whole. I did not realize the piece of me that was missing while it was not with me. It was then it hit me, the entire time I was here, I was not hit with the anxiety I would have felt if I was back in Elswyth without the necklace.

Was there something about this place that made me feel at ease, or was it the man who was now in my company?

"Thank you. You don't know how much this means to me," I whispered.

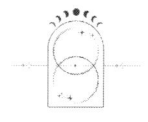

The rest of the day I spent with Violet. She was well aware of the King's plans, and during breakfast she had the royal seamstress fill my room with wedding dresses to choose from. The three of us spent hours trying them on and deciding which I looked best in. After too many dresses to count, I chose an ivory A-line gown with long lace sleeves.

After that, I spent hours getting my hair and make-up done. My ash blonde hair was styled in a low bun, with a few strands hanging loose to frame my face. If the Elder saw my hair like this, she would freak out from the amount of loose strands. However, I felt more beautiful than I ever had. Just as the makeup artist applied the finishing touches on my face, Violet came rushing into the room.

"It's time! It's time!" She squealed.

My heart pounded in my chest. Yes, Malachi and I agreed the marriage would be in ceremony only, but butterflies still filled my stomach at the thought of being his wife. Our conversation from this morning kept replaying in my mind all day. His heart was mine. He opened up to me in such an intimate way, and I could not deny it made my heart flutter. It would take time, but I could see myself giving my heart to him as well.

Violet took my hands in hers and offered me a warm smile. "You are gorgeous. If the King doesn't cry when he sees you, that man has a heart of stone."

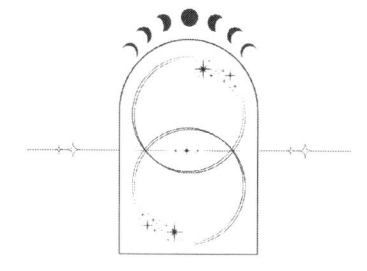

Ten

Outside the castle, facing the city, there was an archway made of white flowers. Under it stood a priest, Artemis, and my soon-to-be husband. My heart skipped a beat as my eyes locked onto his. That familiar pull toward my bridegroom returned, and a warmth washed over me. He had frozen mid-sentence as I came into view, and his jaw fell slack. Artemis used his hand to shut Malachi's mouth for him. Violet's arm was linked with mine as we walked closer to the arch. With each step, my heart pounded in my chest. I reached up and held my pendant, hoping it would bring me some peace.

As we got closer, I saw silver mist in Malachi's eyes. When I first met the king, he seemed so cold. He was to the point with my father, snarky to his guard captain, and gave me the cold shoulder for the first few days I arrived. Something about our conversation from this morning changed the way I looked at him. This man was not cold. He did not have a heart of stone, but a wall he put around it. He only allowed himself to be vulnerable with those he held close.

It was not my necklace that brought me peace in this moment, it was knowing that I was about to wed a good man.

Once we arrived at the arch, it was then I noticed all the fae were in flight, right off the edge of the island. They were all here to watch the wedding between their king and me. It was in that moment it hit me, really hit me. I was marrying a king. Even though I was just brought into this realm, I was about to marry the most important person in theirs. Violet released my arm, bowed gently, and stepped back.

"Wonderful. Let us begin." The priest opened a book and moved, so he now stood on the other side of us, giving the crowd a better view of the bride and groom.

I moved so I was next to Malachi. He looked down at me and smiled. A single tear fell from his eyes, and he quickly wiped it away. "You look beautiful, Ori," he whispered loud enough for only me to hear.

Artemis stood a few steps behind him, and Violet just a few steps behind me.

The priest finally lifted his head from the book and spoke in a language I did not recognize, projecting his voice loud enough for the crowd to hear. After several minutes, he turned his head to Malachi. "Would you like to say a few words, my king?"

"Oriana, I know we have not known each other very long, and this was not how you expected your life to turn out. I made a promise to you this morning. A promise I will now make to you before my entire kingdom. I will do everything in my power to make you happy. Do everything I can to make sure every need and want you have is met." He took in a deep breath and then looked out toward the crowd. "And on this day, I crown you Queen of Aeros. Not consort as many kings before have taken, but queen. My equal in every way. You will always be treated with the same respect I am given. You are free to do as you wish, as any queen does." He looked back at me and smiled.

The crowd cheered, and the priest turned his attention to me. "Oriana, do you have anything you wish to say?"

I swallowed hard. "Malachi, you are right. This is not how I expected my life to go. However, ever since you flew into my life, something felt more right than it ever had. Being in Aeros, I can sense this is where I belong. That these people, your people, are my people. Our people. I promise as Queen, I will do everything I can to do right by them. And I promise to do everything I can to do right by you as your wife." I smiled up at him and stared into his eyes. "My heart belongs to you."

His eyes widened. "Really?" Malachi's voice shook as he spoke.

I nodded in response.

"How beautiful," the priest said. He then continued in the unknown language. After his speech, he looked down at me and smiled. Raising his gaze to Malachi, he spoke again. "You may kiss your bride."

Malachi looked down at me. "Is this ok?" he whispered as he closed the gap between us.

"Kiss me," I whispered back.

A grin crossed his face as he pulled me toward him, leaned down, and gently pressed his lips to mine. Fireworks flashed in my mind. His lips were so soft and warm. I wrapped my arms around his neck and got on my tiptoes to deepen the kiss. His hands slid down to my lower back and held me closer. Too quickly, he pulled his lips away and gave me a longing expression.

"Oriana," he breathed.

Before anyone could say anything else, the ground beneath us rumbled.

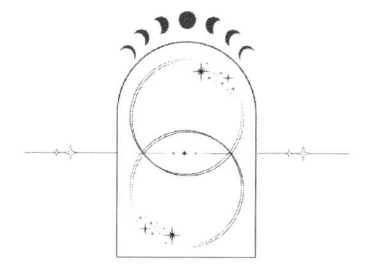

Eleven

My husband released me and staggered forward a few steps to look out toward his people. "Return to the city! Make sure everyone is safe!"

It was then I realized not all in the crowd were civilians. There were several dressed in royal guard uniforms, similar to what Artemis was wearing. The guards from the crowd took off quickly. However, many of our other guests panicked. I could hear them scream about their children and other loved ones as they all flew toward the city.

After a long moment, the quake finally stopped. Violet rushed over to me and wrapped me in a tight embrace. Malachi turned to me with a worried expression and then looked to Artemis.

"Art, I need you to make sure there were no more fallings," he commanded.

"Yes, Sir!"

Before he could take off, the tremors started again, this time much worse than before. Pulling away from Violet, I wobbled and fell to the ground. Malachi called out to me with panic in his voice. He took a step in my direction, and as his foot planted into the ground, it crumbled beneath him. The edge of the island plummeted, and in waves, more land followed. My husband quickly flew upward to avoid following the crumbling land.

Looking up, I noticed that Violet had also fallen to the ground. She was a few feet behind me. The quake abruptly stopped, and before I could stand, the land between the two of us cracked.

My stomach dropped and fear ran through me as I watched the ground split. Firm hands grabbed me, pulling me up. Glancing up in panic, I was relieved to see Malachi. Too quickly, the land disappeared beneath our feet, and the two of us were falling. He held me close to him. The section of the island we were on was breaking into pieces. As Malachi flapped his wings to launch upward, a large hunk of rock slammed into him. I could hear the crunch of bone as Malachi wailed into my ear.

"My King!" Artemis called.

I turned my attention to his voice, and he was diving right for us. Violet was flying just above the island, avoiding the crumbling land. Her eyes were filled with agony and desperation.

Another rock hurled toward us, and Malachi held me tighter and turned his body to protect me from the falling debris.

"Hold on tight, I won't let you fall," he yelled to me.

I clung to him for dear life. My arms were wrapped so tight around his neck that I was worried if I held on any tighter, I would choke him. He grunted as another piece of debris crashed into him. His undamaged wing flapped, trying to fly, but the two of us continued to fall.

Artemis finally made it to our side. Malachi gave him an intense stare. "Take her and get her to safety!"

"My king, I cannot leave you like this." Artemis choked on his words.

"Take her!" Malachi commanded, in the strong voice of a king to his most trusted guard captain. "She is your queen!"

Artemis nodded and extended his arms to take me. As they were transferring me over, another large piece of the island slammed into Malachi's good wing, knocked him off balance, and sent him tumbling. He was forced away, and both of them lost their grip on me, and I began to free fall. I looked up and felt tears flow as I gazed upon the only two men who could save me. A king with two broken wings, and his most trusted friend. A friend who, with the choice of his king or a human woman he just met, would choose his king every time. I could not blame him as I watched Artemis dive for Malachi. Air wooshed around me, and I was too afraid to turn to see how much space was between me and the ground below. So, I looked up and watched as the castle that was to be my home crumbled and fell. No part of the island made it. In a detached thought, I was thankful Violet had gotten away. She was smart enough to fly up before the island started to collapse.

"Are you insane? Go get my queen!" Malachi's screaming pulled me out of my own head. "My wings can heal themselves!"

Artemis dove toward me, dodging the debris. Within a moment, he scooped me up into his arms. "You know, this was not how I pictured the first time I was going to hold you."

Malachi wobbled as he tried to steer himself to us. Somehow, even with his damaged wings, he was able to keep himself from falling to his death.

For the first time, I gained the courage to look down. The ground below was finally visible, and all I could see was the top of a dense forest. The trees were dark green and gray. In the center of the forest, there was a large dead zone, where everything was black. What struck me was seeing the small village in a clearing to the west. To the east, there were four large craters.

"Impossible," Artemis breathed as he hovered in the air, staring at the village.

"Art! Watch out!" Malachi called out from the distance.

Too late.

We turned to see a large piece of debris as it slammed into us. Artemis held me tight, but the two of us tumbled. Unable to catch his balance, we fell below the treetops. His warmth enveloped me as he tried to shield me. We slammed into branches, and after smacking into three of them, Artemis released me. Tears flooded my eyes, as I accepted that I would not survive this fall. My human body would not make it.

My body screamed in pain as another tree branch slammed into my mid-section, but instead of falling to the next one, this branch stopped my decline. I exhaled deeply as the impact stole my breath away.

Artemis continued to tumble until he finally hit the ground and landed on his back about fifty feet below me. He offered me a weak smile as blood leaked from his mouth and nose. The ground around him was littered with chucks of rocks. Finally, he stood, shaking off the daze. He turned away, took a few steps, and looked around. His wings were slumped, and I watched as he writhed in pain as he tried to spread them.

"Are you alright, little one?" He called out to me. "I can barely move my wings, but I will find a way to get you down."

"I..." It was painful to speak, but I forced out the words in a soft voice hoping he could hear me. "I'm in so much pain, but I am alive."

Artemis took a few more steps away from me as he surveyed the scene. He then turned and looked up at me with his head cocked. "Are you able to move at all?"

His eyes went wide and full of fear as the terrifying sound of hundreds of branches snapping filled the air. A guttural scream left my throat as a large piece of land crashed directly on top of Artemis.

Only the tip of his wing was left uncovered. Its white feathers were now red with blood.

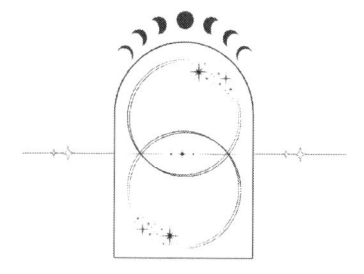

Twelve

I hung from the tree, staring down at the blood that leaked from under the boulder. Tears streamed down my face, and I screamed until my throat was raw. Pain still overwhelmed my body, and I was not able to even attempt to climb down. After Mother knew how long, Malachi came flying through the trees. He was not as fast or stable as he had been in the past but was able to avoid running into any branches. When he said he would heal, he meant it, and I was glad for it.

His eyes locked onto me, and his speed increased. Hovering in the air, he lifted me off the tree limb and held me close to his chest. I buried my head into it and sobbed. His fingers gently went through my hair.

"Darling," he whispered. "It's ok. We made it. You're safe now." His voice trembled. "Where is Artemis?"

Another sob escaped my throat in response.

I felt a gentle thud as Malachi landed. He asked again. "Oriana, where is Artemis?" Fear rattled his voice.

Finally, I was able to lift my head to meet his gaze. Words still refused to leave my throat. Instead, I looked over to the large hunk of land that was to the right. It hit me how little of a chance Artemis had to survive the impact. The boulder was nearly twice as tall as Malachi, and as wide as I was tall.

A cracked whimper escaped Malachi's throat. "No." He pulled me tighter to him and rushed over to the rock. Using one arm, he tried to push the boulder away. It did not budge. "Hold on to me tight. I need to use both hands, and there is no way I am letting you go. I can't lose you, too." Tears flooded his eyes and streamed down his face. I held onto him as tight as I could, and he used both hands to try to push the boulder away. Again, it did not budge. An angered scream escaped his lips.

He tried over and over. Eventually slamming his whole body into it. Nothing he tried worked. After hours passed, he finally gave up. He sat on the ground, held me tight in his lap, and looked down at the wing tip sticking out from the rock. "Artemis, I am so sorry. I am so sorry I could not save you," he sobbed.

Reaching up, I wiped the tears from his eyes. Guilt ran through me. If only my father kept his deal with the fae. Would we have been able to prevent this from happening, or was it my coming here that set off this chain of events?

Malachi's wings sat limp on his back. Normally, he kept them neatly tucked in. Red stained some of the feathers. He grabbed my wrist and pulled it away from his face. "My magic is gone," he said coldly. "With my wings broken, I am not able to fly us back up to Aeros. They healed enough so I could barely fly down here, but they stopped healing. There is something wrong about this place, but I swear to The Mother, I will find a way to get you home safely."

"I saw a town when we were falling," I finally spoke. My throat felt so sore as I forced out the words. "Maybe we could travel there and see if we can find someone who can help us? It's north of here."

Malachi gently took me off his lap and sat me on the ground next to him. Standing, he looked down at me nervously, then to Artemis' wing tip that was peeking from under the rock. He walked over to it and picked off one blood-stained feather and placed it in his breast pocket. Whispering something in the language the priest used during our wedding, he knelt and hung his head, continuing to whisper for a few moments. He then quickly stood and turned to me. Without a word, he scooped me up in his arms and headed north.

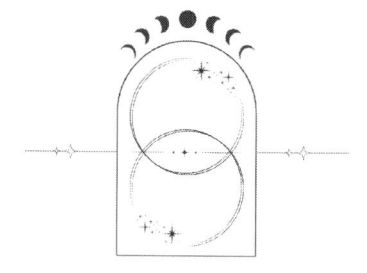

Thirteen

Malachi traveled through the ever-darkening night and kept walking until long after the sun came up. For several hours, I could feel him slowing down, but even as exhaustion crept into him, he never once loosened his grip on me. Neither one of us had spoken a single word during the trek to the unknown village. I found myself slipping in and out of consciousness during the journey. My body and mind had been pushed past their limits. While I was awake, I took in the sights of the evergreen forest. The fresh scent of pine filled my nose.

Finally, the sun began to rise and Malachi allowed himself some rest. He sat under a tree, sat me by his side, and wrapped his wing around me to keep me close. Leaning against him, I closed my eyes and allowed the sun to warm my face. After a while, I opened them to see Malachi looking down at me.

"I am sorry," he said softly.

"You're sorry?" I gave him a confused look.

He nodded. "If I did not keep the terms of the deal, you would not have been put through this. I should have let you stay in the life you knew. The dealings of our fathers had nothing to do with us." He turned his gaze away and looked up at the treetops, which were blocking the view of the sky. Before I could say anything, Malachi jumped up, a growl escaped his throat. "Who's there?"

Five warriors stepped out from behind trees. Each of them wore half masks that resembled birds, and all but one had black masks. The warrior in the center wore a golden mask. They were battle-ready with weapons in hand. Two of them had bows that were loaded and pointed directly at Malachi, and one of the smaller members had their spear pointed at me.

My body tensed as I watched them carefully. Malachi was not in any shape to fight, nor was I. Never had I been in any physical altercation or had weapons pointed at me. The closest thing I had experienced was a small tiff between my sisters and me. Those were bound to happen with close living quarters with multiple women. The one with the golden mask stepped closer, holding his hand up to signal to the others to wait. "It has been a long time since we have seen a winged one. Why have you returned?" he growled.

Malachi stepped closer to him, blocking the path between me and the strangers. "We live above the clouds. The island I called my home collapsed, bringing me and my wife down with it."

Heat rose to my cheeks as I heard him call me his wife. The ceremony was completed moments before the island fell. How could I have forgotten that earth-shattering kiss? I stuffed down those feelings, as now was not the time to wish to feel my husband's lips on mine once again. There was too much at stake.

"We saw a village as we fell. I broke my wings, and we are looking for refuge while I heal. As soon as I am, we will be gone," Malachi continued.

The golden-masked man stared Malachi down for a moment before sidestepping to get a look at me. He chuckled under his breath and shook his head. "A human. You expect me to believe that a fae wed a human? Didn't anyone tell you after you are married you don't need to keep the outfits on?"

It was then I stood, and I inhaled sharply, suppressing a groan as pain shot through my body. It was the first time I moved on my own since before the fall. I did not realize how badly I had been injured from it. Staggering forward to Malachi's side, I snarled at the masked man. "We had just finished the wedding ceremony before the collapse." Rage boiled inside of me. It was one thing after another, and I have had enough. Finally, I allowed myself to feel the pain, the anger, the sadness from everything that had happened since I met the King of Elswyth, and he told me the truth of who I was.

It was then something deep within me clicked. That same powerful sensation I felt during my first training session was now one with me. As if it had been there my entire life, my magic flowed through my veins. "We mean you no harm. Look at us! We clearly pose no threat. So lower your weapons and help my husband!" I commanded. If I needed to, I would use my magic to destroy anyone who opposed us.

I was a threat, and I prayed they could not feel the power I now sensed within myself. I would not hesitate to explore the extent of it if I was pushed to do so.

The golden-masked man pulled it from his face and cocked his head as he examined me. His eyes went wide as they trailed down my body and stopped at my neckline. "Stand down!" He called to his warriors.

Malachi once again moved to protect me from these warriors, this time, pulling me close to his side. "Why are you looking at her like that?"

"That necklace. Where did you get it?" he asked quickly.

One of the bow-wielders stepped forward to their leader's side and removed her mask. "Necklace? Since when do you care about jewelry from above? Let's bring them into the Elder and allow him to decide their fate."

"Silence, Katerina!" He turned and snarled at her. "I care when the necklace looks exactly like the Calamita."

The other warriors let out a gasp, and the second bowman pointed his weapon at me.

The Calamita? What the hell was that, and why did it cause a reaction from these people?

"I advise you to remove your aim from my wife. If not, I will tear you limb from limb." A deep and guttural growl escaped his throat.

I could not help but swoon over how protective this man was over me. Mother, help me. The vows I made to her were going to be nearly impossible to keep. The more time I spent with my husband, the less I wanted to keep the vows with The Mother. I just prayed she would forgive me when the time came.

"The necklace. Where did you get it? I won't ask again," the gold-masked warrior snarled.

"It's a family heirloom. It belonged to my mother before she died. What is Calamita? And why do you think I have it?"

The leader turned to the bowman and ordered him to lower his weapon before looking at me again. "We will take you to the village where The Elder can tell you all about it. My name is Karjo. I am the Elder's son." He turned his attention towards my husband. "No one in our village has wings, as they are all cut off at birth. However, our healer comes from a long line of healers. She may have some journals from before that will guide her on how to heal your wings."

"Why would you cut off your wings?" Hurt radiated from Malachi's voice.

"No need to have them if we cannot fly. We have not flown since the last king rose the capitol into the sky and left us to deal with what he created."

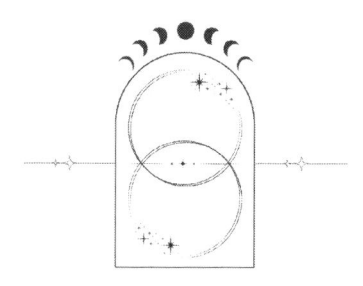

Fourteen

We walked in silence as we made our way to the village. Other than Karjo, the other four warriors refused to even speak to us as if we were beneath them, and Katerina kept her hand on her blade at all times. They did not trust us, but could I blame them? Based on the last thing Karjo said about what we know as the Great Calamity, they did not have a good last impression of Malachi's ancestors.

His last words kept repeating in my mind. What did he mean when he said it was the king who created it? Did Malachi's family have something to do with whatever had happened, and did he know more than he led on? Surely, the history of the royal family would be passed down from generation to generation.

Though, out of anyone, I should understand how easy it is for royals to keep secrets. I was the King of Elswyth's best-kept secret for twenty-five years. Was I still a secret to everyone but my two sisters and the Elder? Thinking about them hurt my heart. How I missed them so, for they were my family, not the king. He may be my blood, but blood was not what made family.

Family was formed by bonds of trials. It was the Elder who raised me. It was my sisters who made me feel loved and cherished. It was my father who made me feel like I was nothing. That all I was, was a dark secret that soiled the royal family name. Only good to be sold to the fae as a pawn in a war that had not yet come to our shores.

The forest did not get any less dense as we continued our walk. It was a few hours before we reached the village. The buildings were all made of pale logs. If it was snowing, it would remind me of a winter solstice greeting card. All eyes were on us as we walked through the village. The fae here looked like the fae from Aeros, minus the wings. Some of the elders even had white tattoos that mimicked my husbands. Karjo dismissed the warriors, but Katerina stayed with us. Taking us to the center of town, Karjo led us to a large building that overlooked the square.

"Father," he called out, "I brought guests that you will be very interested in meeting."

"I am in my office," a deep voice called out from the back of the building.

Karjo guided us through the halls and into the Elder's office. Katerina stood guard in the doorway, her hand still on her blade, blocking our exit.

The Elder looked up from his desk, and eyes went wide as he met Malachi's gaze. "It has been a long time since someone with wings has been to this village alive." He stood from his seat, walked around to the front of his desk, and leaned against it. "How did you make it down here without dying?"

"Why would you kill the fae we sent here?" Malachi snarled. "We just wanted to know the state of the land after The Calamity!"

The Elder shook his head. "You misunderstand me. They did not touch the ground with life in their veins. Magic has been gone from this land for years. Once they flew too far from the raised lands, they lost their ability to fly, and that was a long fall. So, I will ask again, how were you able to fly all the way down, and can you still?"

The room fell silent. Nervously, I looked around at everyone as tension built. Malachi tightened his jaw before he spoke. "I do not know how we were able to make it, but the others didn't. As for me flying now, no. My wings are broken. Debris hit them as I fell, and they partially healed, but not enough for me to fly myself and my wife back to the sky."

"Father, I believe I know how they made it. Ever since I have been near the human, I could feel a tingle in my core, just as the olden ones said. Just being close to her calls for my magic to return. Look upon her neck, is that the Calamita?" Karjo interjected.

The Elder then looked at me. His eyes widened. "That necklace. Let me see it, please."

"Do not give it to him," Malachi snapped. He extended his arm out in front of me to create a barrier between the Elder and myself.

Holding on tight to the pendant, I looked at my husband nervously. These people were not exactly hostile, but I was not sure if I could trust them. But, they could be the only chance we have to find a way back above the clouds.

"I will give it back on my honor. I simply want to examine it for a moment. We can make a deal if that will make you feel better."

Fae deals could not be backed out of. I knew that better than anyone. The fact he even offered calmed my nerves slightly. I looked up at Malachi and he offered one nod, lowering his arm. Knowing he thought it was okay gave me comfort in my decision. Removing the necklace, I extended it out to the Elder. When his hands touched it, he recoiled with a hissing sound, as if it burned him.

"Father! Are you ok?" Karjo rushed over to him.

The Elder raised his hand. "I am fine, Son. That definitely is the Calamita. Human, where did you get that?"

"It was my mother's, according to my father. She died in childbirth. I never met her."

"Was she a sorceress, by any chance?" The Elder raised an eyebrow.

I hesitated for a moment. Scared of what this all meant, I wasn't sure if I should be honest. But if I wasn't, would we ever get the answers we needed? They also have not given us any reason to distrust them. Best not to give them a reason to distrust us. "She was. I am as well."

The Elder shot his gaze to Malachi. "I assume you want to reunite the sky and land?"

"I do more than anything," he responded.

"Do you think the sky king is fair? Would he try to conquer us?" The Elder asked in a firm tone.

"I am the sky king if that is what you wish to call me. However, I call myself the King of Aeros." Malachi hardened his gaze on the Elder. "Is this Aeros?"

"This land has not been called that for many years. We call our land Teros. Teros has no king. This village is the only one remaining in all the land. We govern through the people. Yes, while I am the Elder, we have a council, and our citizens vote on issues." The Elder narrowed his gaze.

I had never heard of a land with no king, or one that allows for its people to vote on how things should be run. I found the idea fascinating.

"I see no reason to change that. I am no conqueror. I wish the best for my people," Malachi said with a smile. "Perhaps Aeros may adopt the Teros ways once we are reunited."

If I did not think that I was falling for the fae king, I knew now. He truly wanted what was best for the people, and not just his people, but the people here as well. Many would see a king relinquishing his power as a weakness. However, I saw it as one of his many strengths.

"Perhaps you can sit upon the council. But that is all in good time. We can talk about that after the task you need to complete is done."

"We are in no condition to go on any quests!" I motioned over to Malachi. "His wings need to be healed. I feel like I am going to collapse at any moment!" However, to be honest, ever since I felt myself become one with my magic, the pain throughout my body lessened. Exhaustion had still seeded itself in my core.

"And rest you shall. For where I am about to send you, you will need to be in top shape. Come with me, for this is a story that needs to be told, and would be much better if you were sitting." The Elder walked out of his office, and Katerina and Karjo followed him out of the room. Malachi and I then left as well. Taking us to a sitting room, the Elder motioned for us to sit on an orange loveseat. We sat, and Malachi immediately pulled me close to him. As like in the Elder's office. Katerina still stood in the doorway, blocking our exit. Karjo and the Elder sat on the couch across from us.

"Long ago, before Aeros was raised to the sky, we all lived in harmony. Until a sorceress from Elswyth traveled here, looking for help. She had spent all of her power trying to save her sister from Orilon. At least that's what she told the King. However, she turned out to be a liar. She did not want to save her sister, she wanted to control her. She used much of her magic to curse Orilon and needed her magical well replenished. Being just a man, the King was powerless to the damsel in distress she presented herself as. In the center of the forest, stood an obelisk that was the core of our magic. Our king took her there, as he had fallen for her ruse. Before the king knew it, she stole from the obelisk and ripped the magic from our realm."

I could not believe what I was hearing. It was my ancestors who caused all of this. Not only this, but they cursed another realm as well. Maybe my father was right. Could sorceresses not be trusted? Would the magic corrupt me? Would I end up doing horrible things as well?

As if Malachi could sense my anxiety, he pulled me in tighter, gently rubbing my shoulder. "You would never be capable of such horrible deeds," he whispered so softly that I could barely hear him.

"To escape the spread of magic loss, the king rose the capital into the sky, leaving us here, empty. Many of the remaining fae did not survive without our magic. The ones who did survive were left feeling like husks as if we were not whole beings. I am sure you understand the feeling since I am sure you also cannot feel your magic as you once did above."

"I feel as if half of my soul has withered. Without my magic, I feel less than fae," Malachi said somberly.

"That is how my people have felt since birth. Now the two of you have the chance to correct your ancestors' wrongs. Once you are healed, you will travel to the center of the forest, restore the magic into the obelisk, and set our people free."

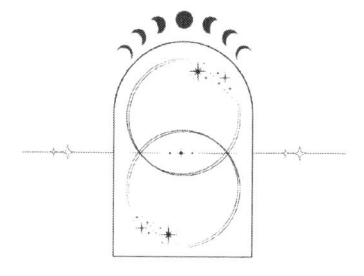

Fifteen

We had been in Teros for three days. As soon as we were finished with the Elder, Karjo took us to a small empty cottage at the edge of the village. Even after we went inside to settle in and rest, Katerina was never too far away. I constantly saw her keeping an eye on us.

On our first night, the healer had come by and set Malachi's wings so they would heal properly. In doing so, she had to break them again and move them into the correct position. I hated hearing his screams. Once his wings were set, I sat at his bedside, watching him. Gently, I ran my fingers up and down his back in between his wings. I pledged to myself that never again would he scream in pain.

My wounds, however, had mostly healed. My skin was left bruised, but most of the internal damage fixed itself. I could not help but wonder if it was me that was doing this, or if it was the magic of the Calamita.

The two of us stayed in separate rooms, but part of me wished he would knock on my door just once to ask if he could stay with me. I was not sure how much I would be ready for romantically, but I wanted to sleep in the arms of the one man who made me feel safe. I could not understand how in such a short amount of time, I had fallen for a man who I dreaded marrying. It made my heart flutter knowing he had fallen for me, too.

The Mother answered my prayers when I heard a soft knock on the door to my bedroom. I jolted up, the covers fell into my lap.

"Ori, are you up?" Malachi asked through the door.

"Come in!" I called out in response.

The door slowly opened, revealing Malachi shirtless, and in long sleep trousers. I focused on the white geometric patterns that were inked on his skin. My eyes trailed down his body and I bit my lower lip. A playful smirk grew across his face.

"Oh, like what you see, do you?" he asked in a teasing tone.

Heat flooded my cheeks, and I looked down into my lap. How bold have I gotten since meeting the fae man who turned my entire life upside down? Before I could say anything, he continued to speak.

"I wanted to tell you that my wings are all better. Whenever you are ready, we can start our journey to the center of the forest." He came over and sat on the edge of my bed. Gently, he lifted my chin to make our eyes meet. "I didn't mean to embarrass you. I apologize for that."

"It's ok. This whole thing is not something that I am used to," I said softly. In such a short time my life had completely changed. If you asked me just a few weeks ago, I would have told you that I would never marry. I would have told you I would never be in a room with a shirtless man.

But yet, here I was. It would be a lie to say I wasn't enjoying it.

"Well, at least you aren't alone in that. Neither am I."

I cocked my head and raised my brow. "What do you mean?"

He took my hands in his. "I have waited my whole life to meet you. Never once did I stray."

"Never?" When I first arrived, Artemis made it seem like the exact opposite had been going on, so I was very confused.

Malachi chuckled nervously and looked away. "Never."

"But Art—" I began, but Malachi quickly cut me off.

"He was just trying to ruffle my feathers. He liked to do that."

My heart ached at the use of past tense. In the little time I had known Artemis, he had become a good friend. Even though he tried to save his friend and king first, it was *my* life he saved.

And in doing so, lost his own.

Malachi gently wiped his thumb under my eyes, removing the tears that had fallen. "He would not want us to be sad. He would want us to continue on this quest and save our people. We will have time to give him the ceremony he deserves. For now, we need to save our energy on what is ahead," he whispered as he leaned forward and pressed his forehead to mine.

We sat there for a long moment in silence, staring into each other's eyes. The air electrified around us. I was not sure who made the first move, as it all happened too quickly. Our lips collided in fiery passion. Malachi moved forward, causing me to lie on my back as he got on top of me, our kiss never breaking. This was even more magical than the kiss that sealed our vows. Fireworks exploded inside me as our tongues danced.

My body yearned for more as he pulled away, but he only did so to remove the blanket from me. He tossed it to the floor, and a smirk grew on his face as he drank in the sight of me.

"Who knew you would go to bed in something so sexy?" he purred.

I wore a simple white silk slip. It was something very similar that I had worn back at the sanctuary. Never had I considered it sexy. Looking back, I was the only one who chose to wear something like this. My sisters all had worn longer nightgowns with sleeves.

Reaching up, I toyed with the thin strap. "I'm glad you like it," I purred back.

"Darling, I don't want you to do anything that you are not ready for. Let me know if you want me to stop at any point."

I thought about it for a moment. How far did I want to take this with my husband? Somehow, knowing he waited for me for all these years made me want him even more. Again, I struggled with the vows I made to The Mother. However, I broke many of those vows. Sisters were not to take a husband. The promise of my hand had been made long before I made my vows to The Mother. I had also made vows to this man during our wedding.

For once, I needed to stop worrying about what others expected of me and do what felt right in my heart. I loved The Mother, but when I made my vows to her, everything seemed so wrong, as if I was trapped within the walls of the sanctuary. When I stood in front of

Malachi and vowed to be his wife and give him a chance to win my heart, I felt free.

"Go slow, but don't stop," I finally said softly.

"Are you sure?" he asked again.

I nodded in response and his lips were on mine once more. His hands slid down and found their way to my side as he pushed up my nightgown, exposing my underwear. His fingers trailed down to my core and gently rubbed against the small piece of cloth that I was now so angry at for existing. I didn't want anything between us. Wetness pooled in my center, and I craved more of his touch. A moan escaped my lips. I reached down and tried to remove Malachi's pants, but he grabbed my arms and pinned them to the bed.

Pulling away from my lips, he growled, "Not yet, my queen." Slowly, he removed my underwear, exposing my bare sex to him. His fingers slowly teased my slit, just barely entering me. When he pulled away his fingers, they glistened with my wetness, and when he dragged his tongue across his fingers, he let out a groan. "Delicious."

Lowering his head, his tongue grazed across the most intimate part of me. I arched my back and let out a soft moan in response. Never had I experienced anything like this, but I trusted Malachi fully and I knew I was in good hands. Flicking against my sensitive clit, his tongue found ways to drive me wild. Never did I expect to feel so much pleasure. He removed his tongue from me, and I pleaded for more. I never wanted him to stop.

"Oh, darling. That was a warm-up. The fun has just begun," he teased.

I thanked the gods when he finally removed his own pants. My eyes went wide as his considerable length sprang free.

"Are you still ok? You're sure you want me to continue?" He asked nervously.

My core melted. He was so considerate of me and my feelings, and it only made me want him more. "Please," I pleaded.

"As you wish." He spread my legs and situated himself in between them. His tip was so close to my aching core, but yet so far away at the same time. I thanked The Mother when it prodded my entrance. Slowly, he pushed it in, and as I stretched to accommodate him, another moan escaped my lips.

Slowly, he eased in and out of me, and each time, he went a little deeper. Pleasure coursed through my body, and I cried out wordlessly. He leaned forward and kissed me hard as he thrust in as deep as he could. As I kissed him back, I truly thought I was in paradise. His pace increased, and I felt him hit the deepest part of me over and over.

My body teetered on an edge I didn't know existed. I was so close to exploding, but Malachi fully removed himself.

"Not yet," he growled. His cock slapped against my opening firmly before he pushed it back inside. Holding onto my hips, he slammed into me, this time not holding back, and I screamed in pleasure. I was so glad we had this cottage to ourselves. Hopefully, no one outside could hear us. Malachi groaned as he pushed himself in and held it there.

"Please, don't stop," I begged.

"Oh, darling. The next time I go, I won't stop until you have exploded, and I have filled you with my essence. Do you understand? Is that what you want?"

"Please!"

Malachi flipped me over, so I was on my hands and knees. With his hands firmly holding my hips, he plowed himself back into me. I did not think it was possible to have him deeper, but he was proving me wrong. My eyes rolled into the back of my head as I fell to my elbows.

"Grip the headboard," he commanded.

Reaching up, I obeyed. My hands held onto the wood as he fucked me from behind. I felt myself tighten around him and my body quivered. Pleasure continued to build within me, and I felt as if I could explode.

"Cum for me, darling," he purred.

At that moment, worlds collided, were destroyed and rebuilt. Never in my life had I had such an experience.

"Good girl." He leaned down and nibbled my ear, slowing down his thrust, making sure I felt everything as he pounded into me. Holding himself deep inside of me, my husband let out a deep groan. He twitched, and I felt something hot deep in my core. He did not stop thrusting, even as he filled me. "Mine," he growled. "Oriana, you are mine. Forever."

"Forever," I moaned back. "And you are mine."

"Darling, I have been yours since I first laid eyes on you." He slowly removed himself, and his essence dripped from me. He got out of the bed and lifted me into his arms. "Let's get cleaned up, then we can sleep in my bed tonight."

"Sounds perfect." I smiled up at him.

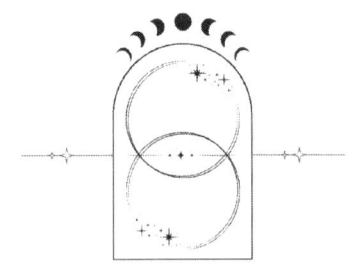

Sixteen

Two days later, Malachi and I were on our journey to the center of the forest. Karjo provided us with vague directions but insisted it should only take us about a full day's walk to get there. Apparently, no one had traveled too far from the village in decades, and little was known about what awaited us. His last words to us were a word of warning.

The last people who traveled to the center of the forest had not returned. Though fear had settled into my core, Malachi promised that we would be different from the others. We would do what needed to be done and save our people.

We traveled for hours, and I was thankful Malachi allowed me to walk. He stayed a couple of paces behind me, ready to strike if need be. To our surprise, the forest was still and silent. Not even bird song ran through these woods. The eerie silence gave me no solace. Over time, the green pines shifted into petrified wood. Many of the trees were shriveled as if the life had been sucked from them. All of them were barren of leaves, nor was there any evidence that leaves had ever been here. This cold place was truly desolate.

"We can take a break if you need to," Malachi said as he caught up to me and walked by my side.

Looking up at him, I let out a huff. "Just because I am human does not mean I am weak."

"I did not say that. I am concerned about you. We have traveled for miles, and you have yet to slow down." He took my hand and stopped walking.

This caused me to stop, so I turned to face him. "Mal, I promise you I am fine."

"Mal?" He smirked down at me. "I like that I'm getting nicknames."

"Want to hear another one I have for you?" I smirked back and pressed my body against his. "Pain in my ass."

He threw his head back and laughed. "Mother, you are fcisty."

Before I could respond, a blood-curdling scream rang through the forest. Malachi pulled me close to him and lifted me off the ground. Thankfully, now that the healer fixed his wings, Malachi could fly once again. With a flap of his wings, he launched us into the sky, above the treetops. Clinging to him, I looked below to see what could have made the sound. It was not long before my eyes landed on one of the most horrifying things I had ever seen. This humanoid creature had skin as white as snow, red eyes, long claws and fangs, and large bat-like wings.

"W—what is that?" I whimpered.

"That, my dear, is one of the cursed fae of Orilon. I saw them firsthand when I attended their king's wedding. The fact one of them is here proves the Elder right. The witch who cursed Orilon is also the one who stole magic from our land."

The creature looked up and screamed again once its sights were on us. It launched itself into the air with breakneck speed. Long, blood-stained claws swiped at us. Malachi dodged its attack.

"I still can't feel my magic. This one is all on you!" Mal called to me.

Panic filled my veins. Even though I could sense my magic, I still never used it, or really even knew how to use it. I still had no idea what I could do. The Calamita grew warm around my neck as if an answer to my prayers. This necklace held the magic of the land. From what I knew, the fae of Aeros all had gravitational magic. I would use the magic from this land to my advantage. Focusing on pulling magic from the stone, heat filled my body, and built up within me, and begged for release.

I was not sure how I did it, but I felt my magic set free. As it was released, comforting heat flooded my body. The cursed fae slammed into the ground, letting out another scream on impact. Malachi flew lower, getting us a better view of the creature. It refused to die from the fall, and staggered up off the ground, letting out a hiss. Before it could take a step, I focused on my magic again. It released from me, and in one swift motion, the cursed fae's neck snapped, and its body fell to the ground. This time, it did not get back up.

Malachi landed next to the fae, still holding me in his arms. We stayed silent for a moment until he chuckled softly. "My wife is so badass."

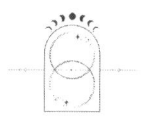

After the attack, we decided to take a short rest. After the huge burst of power, I had gained a headache from the amount of magic I had expelled. Mal informed me that there was a delicate balance when it came to using magic. If too much was used, one could easily burn out and be powerless for some time until the magical well refilled. Once we were well rested, we started the journey once again and did not stop until we reached the obelisk. Malachi flew us most of the way to make the journey go by faster. Everything looked the same as we traveled through the petrified wood. I was beginning to think we were going in circles until out of seemingly nowhere what we were searching for appeared. It was as if some form of magic camouflaged it until we got closer. The pure white obelisk sat in the center of a small clearing. My gaze followed its full length above the trees. The Calamita stone in my necklace throbbed against my skin. It got more intense with each step I took, closer to the obelisk.

Malachi stayed close behind me as I approached the obelisk. There was a small hole that matched the shape of my piece of the Calamita. I removed it from my neck and looked up toward the opening. Tightening my grip on the stone, worry filled my head. What if once I restored the magic to the obelisk, I lost all of mine? Even though this was a new part of me, my heart ached at the thought of losing it. The magic was mine; it was given to me by my family. Why should I give it back to the land who threw it away?

It was then I realized the voice in my head was not one I recognized. Still feminine, but it was cold and raspy. I shook my head hard to try to clear those thoughts. As I extended my arm to place the Calamita in its spot, it felt as if my body was fighting against me. Like there was another force preventing me from completing my task. Falling to my knees, I let out a scream as the excruciating pain of burning fire replaced the magic in my veins.

Malachi rushed to my side and knelt. "Oriana! What is wrong?"

I looked up at him and opened my mouth to speak, but no words came out. Instead, I forced myself to hand him the Calamita and pointed to the indent in the obelisk.

With a nod, he took it and held it tight. How he was able to hold it, but the other fae couldn't, I would never understand. It was just another sign from The Mother proving that we were meant to be.

Another wave of pain crashed into me, I curled in on myself, and I let out another wail. My gaze never left Malachi, even as the fire within got worse. With determination all over his face, he slammed the Calamita into the obelisk, and bright light filled my vision.

The pain instantly vanished, leaving no trace of it. When the flash cleared and my vision returned to normal, the surrounding trees were now green and full of life. Malachi ran back over to me and helped me stand. The clouds in the sky vanished, and the sun warmed our skin. Joy surged through me until Malachi looked up, and horror washed over his face.

Matching his gaze, I saw the three remaining islands of Aeros falling toward the ground.

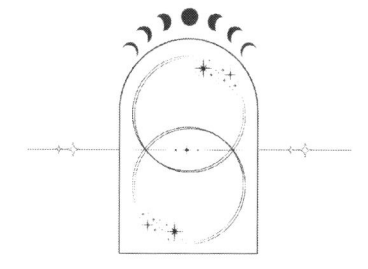

Seventeen

Malachi launched himself into the air, flying as fast as he could toward the islands. Too quickly were they approaching the land. Unlike when the castle fell, these were not crumbling or falling apart. No, three massive pieces of earth were careening toward the ground. The force would be enough to ruin the land below, and I could not help but wonder what other effects it would have on the entire land of Teros. Not only that, but the city would not survive the impact. Where would any survivors go? Would there even be any survivors?

The King of Aeros began to undo what his great-grandfather did long ago. I could sense his magic in the air. It was a large force that weighed down on me. Forcing myself to stand, I watched as he used his magic to try to stop the islands from crashing. The tattoos on his skin glowed and I swore that I could see the streams of magic wrapping around the base of the island and pulling upwards. They slowed, but not enough to make a difference. Horror continued to fill me. If the most powerful fae of Aeros could not stop them, who could? I wondered if I kept my magic, instead of giving it back to the land, would I have been able to help him?

Power radiated from the obelisk. The spot where Malachi slammed the Calamita in place was now fully fused. It was impossible to tell if a piece was ever missing. The heaviness I was feeling from Malachi's magic seemed to lift off me. It was replaced with something else.

A calling to the obelisk.

An overwhelming sensation washed over me, demanding I touch it. Unable to ignore its call, I rushed over to it and placed my palm against the warm white stone.

Like when Malachi touched the obelisk, a bright flash of light flooded my vision. When it cleared, I was no longer standing in the middle of a forest. I was now in a throne room with the most beautiful white marble columns.

"It has been a long time since a sorceress has been in my halls," an unfamiliar feminine voice rang from behind me. It was the most beautiful sound I had ever heard.

When I spun to see who was there, I immediately fell to my knees and bowed. Pressing my forehead to the cold marble floor, embarrassment washed over me. My entire life was spent worshiping the goddess that stood before me. Here I was, in dirty travel clothes and my vows for her forsaken.

"My Goddess," I finally managed to say, "it is an honor to be in your presence." My entire body trembled.

She let out a soft laugh. "Please rise, child."

I did as she said, wiping off the front of me as I got off the ground. I refused to meet her gaze, for I did not deserve to look into her eyes.

"You have spent your entire life trying to live in a way that would please me." Her tone was soft, yet commanding. "You have done well by your sisters, your family, and your husband. Yet, you believe yourself to be a disappointment? Why is this? Look me in the eye as you tell me, child."

Slowly, I raised my gaze. Her soft green eyes were filled with an emotion I could not determine. "I made a vow to save myself. I made promises that I did not keep."

She laughed again. "Child, you think I care about that? You think I care who you lie with, or how often? Tell me, how many children do I have?"

"Twelve."

She stepped closer to me. Grabbing my chin, she forced me to stay my gaze. "You do not get twelve children by remaining pure. Your teachers tell you they are all sired by the same man. That is a lie. Some have no father, and some share the same. Hell, I have even been with a woman since the realms split. Please do not feel ashamed to show love and passion however you see fit, especially not with a man who I chose for you."

"You chose him for me?" I raised an eyebrow.

She finally released me and took a step back. "Yes. Everything has been laid out as it should be. I am also offended you would believe I would send you on a quest to sacrifice yourself in the end. Women are not to be used and disposed of. Yes, the magic needed to be restored to the land. But the power in that necklace was never yours. It was a tool to help you unlock yours that was sealed away. Now, return to Aeros, call upon your power, and help the man you love."

On her last word, another flash of light filled my vision, and when it cleared, I was back in the clearing. Looking up to Malachi, I saw little change since the first flash. It was as if no time passed at all. Finally, I felt the magic flowing through my veins.

The Mother was right. It was never gone, it had just become one with me. So natural I could now feel its presence in everything I did.

Focusing hard on my magic, the air electrified around me. I followed the motions my husband was performing. Pretty soon, the islands slowed and were in our control. Malachi flew down to meet back up with me.

"Whatever you are doing, keep it up. The islands are now stable." He pulled me into his arms and launched us back into the sky. Now that the islands were no longer plummeting, fae filled the air around us. They, too, lent their magic to help us guide the islands back into the craters they were ripped from centuries ago.

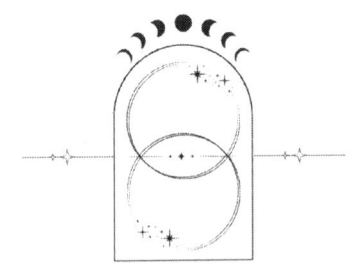

Eighteen

Two months passed since Aeros returned to the land. With the castle gone, Malachi and I moved into a penthouse in the city. He had been busy coordinating with the village elder to reunite Aeros and Teros. The first part in that plan was Malachi stepping down as king, and he joined the council that now ruled both people. The people of Aeros did not really understand the new ways, but they seemed to accept them. They still referred to Malachi as king, to many of them he would always be the king in their hearts. For he had earned it by saving them all.

Violet was so happy both Malachi and I were alright. She and I had been spending every day with each other, and the two of us created a group that met once a week to discuss the teachings of The Mother. Both citizens of Teros and Aeros attended. It was a great way to reconnect the people.

I still could not believe I had the honor of meeting The Mother. Her words would play through my mind for the rest of my days.

I was not a one-time use creature to save the realm, and then to be disposed of.

I continued my work with Malachi to help keep our people happy. Even though my title as Queen did not last long, the people of Aeros still saw me as theirs, and I would do everything in my power not to disappoint them.

Ever since returning, we had not gotten a chance to give Artemis the ceremony he deserved. Tonight, that would change. His loved ones, members of the guard, and citizens of Aeros all gathered in a field just outside the city where a pyre had been lit in his honor.

One by one, people told stories of Artemis, stories of his time in the guard, and what he was like as a young fae. He would be missed dearly.

Malachi was the last to speak. He walked toward the flame, then turned toward the crowd. "Artemis served by my side since we were young boys. He did not want to be my bodyguard, but his father was guard captain under my father's rule. They thought it would be best for both of us if he was assigned that role. One night, we snuck out of the castle, went to the portal island, and glamoured ourselves into humans. We found ourselves on a small island, and we stayed there for three days. We got into so much trouble when we returned." He let out a little chuckle and wiped the silver mist from his eyes. "The first night I brought Oriana into this realm, he invited himself to our lunch. When she returned to her room, he told me that if I did not marry her, he would. Gods, how I wish he could see what change she has brought to our lands. He would be over the moon."

Malachi dug into his pocket and pulled out the single feather. It was now dark brown from the aged blood that stained it. He turned to the fire and released it. As he spoke words in an unknown language, the feather danced on the wind until it joined the flames. The fire roared and embers floated on the breeze.

We all stayed until the fire died out. Malachi made his way through the crowd of people, continuing the conversations about how Artemis would be missed. When he made it to my side, he wrapped his arm around my shoulders. "Well, dear wife, are you ready for me to fly us home? Sorry, we stayed so late. I know you must be exhausted."

I gave a small yawn before answering. "I understand. Please do not feel like you have to rush on my account."

He leaned in and placed a gentle kiss on my lips. "There is nothing more I want than to return home and crawl into my bed with my wife."

Pressing my body into his, I smiled up at him. "Well, by all means, don't let me stop you."

The End

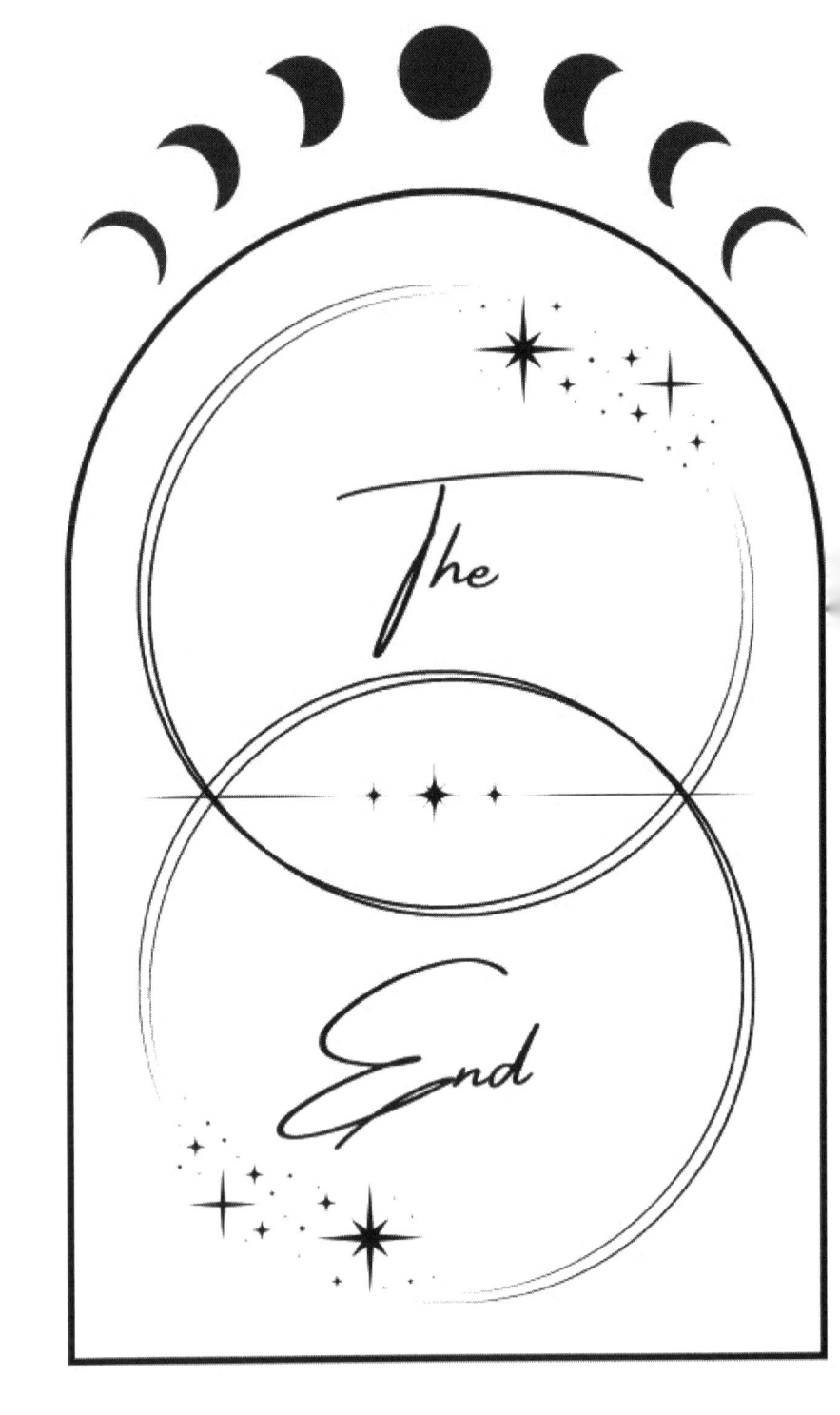

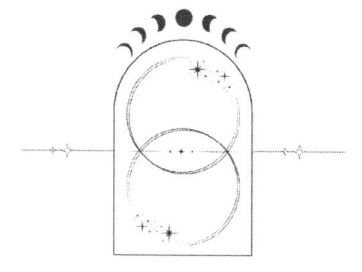

Also by Willow Asteria

The Blood Singer Trilogy
https://amzn.to/3KO4erc

The Realms of Elswyth
https://amzn.to/3xsvM2r

Learn More Here!

Made in the USA
Middletown, DE
08 March 2025